Defending Elena
A True North Ranch Story

MOUNTAINS &
MAGNOLIAS
PUBLISHING

Defending Elena
A True North Ranch Story

By: TESSA LEIGH

Printed in the United States of America.

For information address Tessa Leigh, 923 Oldham Drive, PO Box 384, Nolensville, TN 37135

Published by: Mountains & Magnolias Publishing

Amazon ISBN: 979-8-9991894-0-0

ISBN: 979-8-2830647-0-3

First Edition May 2025

DEFENDING ELENA

DEDICATION

To my own Veteran,

Thank you for your service and for supporting my adventures in writing.

Love you!

Tessa

ACKNOWLEDGMENTS

For my Dad:

A veteran, a rancher, and the truest adventurer I've ever known. Thank you for showing us how to dream with our feet on the ground and our hearts wide open. Your imagination lit the trail, allowing us to find and build our own adventures.

And to every reader chasing something brave and true...
May you always find your true north.

TABLE OF CONTENTS

Chapter 1

Hidden Truths

JACK

The smell hits me first, sawdust, sweat, and animal musk all baking under the midday sun. It's loud, too. Voices bark out bids, boots clomp against packed dirt, and somewhere a kid cries over a melted snow cone. Typical auction day chaos. I'm standing near the holding pens, my boots caked in dust, laser-focused on a brindle steer I've had my eye on all morning. He's sturdy. Temperamental. The kind of stock that keeps a man's ranch sharp.

"Seven-fifty!" someone yells.

I counter without hesitation, "Eight hundred!"

It's instinct. Numbers. Weight. Feed-to-gain ratio. Things that make sense. Not like the woman standing across the arena.

I spot her between a cowboy hat and a swinging gate. Her long blonde hair, dark jeans, tension in her shoulders like she's braced for a blow. Elena Dawson. My dead partner's widow. The woman I swore I'd never see again. The last person I want to see.

My pulse spikes, but not in any way I like.

What the hell is she doing here?

She's scanning the crowd like she's looking for someone, or running from them. I turn away fast, ducking my head and adjusting my hat. Not supposed to be my problem. Not anymore.

But fate's got other ideas.

There's a commotion near the pens. The sounds of snorting, shouting, and someone yelling, "Gate's not latched!" That gets my attention. A blur of brown muscle bursts loose as a steer breaks free, barreling straight through the crowd.

People scream and scatter. The auctioneer's voice is swallowed by the chaos. I jump the fence, instinct kicking in before I can think.

And then I see her. Elena. Frozen. Right in the steer's path.

"Move!" I bark, but she doesn't.

Damn it.

I bolt toward her.

Doing a quick assessment, I see cowboys scrambling. Some are moving small kids, some are yelling to lock the gates, but I clock a saddled horse tied off at the post, standing calm in the chaos.

In three strides, I've got the reins in hand and I'm talking to the horse like we're old friends. "Let's go catch us a steer."

I swing up fast, grab the horn, and we're off! The saddle's already cinched tight, thank God. No hesitation. He's a solid animal. Muscle, speed, no fear, and he tunes in like he knows exactly what I need. I don't know who he belongs to, but he's a damn fine horse. We close the gap fast on the steer that's causing all the panic.

We're feet away when I spot her.

Elena.

Still frozen. Eyes wide, shoulders locked. Like she's not even in her body.

I can't stop the steer in time.

I make a snap decision and kick the horse as we pivot toward her. He responds like a pro, launching us forward.

She sees me. I see her. Everything narrows to that one breath.

I reach down, bracing with my left leg and gripping the reins tight, and swoop low off the saddle. She moves in perfect sync, reaching up. My arm reaches across her chest, my hand wrapped under her arm for leverage, she uses the momentum to swing herself up behind me.

She's safe.

I angle the reins hard to the right and we veer away from the path of the rampaging steer. He's headed toward open space now, and two other cowboys are giving chase. Let them deal with it. I've got something more important behind me.

I slow the horse to a steady walk as we head back toward the barn. Her arms wrapped around my middle, her body pressed close. I can feel the heave of her breath, fast and shallow, against my back.

"You okay back there?" I ask, voice lower than I mean it to be.

She doesn't answer right away. Then, with a voice tight and shaking just enough to make my chest squeeze, she says, "Ask me when we find my heart on the ground."

We dismount near the hitching post close to where it all started. Elena slides off behind me and lands less gracefully than I expect, her knees buckling a little. I catch her elbow on instinct.

She jerks away like my touch burns. "I'm fine."

Could've fooled me. Her face is pale, and she's doing that thing where she is looking everywhere but at me, like if she doesn't meet my eyes, the history between us won't matter.

"You always show up places where you're not supposed to be?" I ask, tugging the reins over the post. I try to sound casual, but my voice comes out harder than I meant.

She crosses her arms. "You always play cowboy hero? That wasn't exactly subtle."

"You were about to get trampled, Elena. Forgive me for not waiting to send a written invitation."

The sarcasm in her eyes fades just enough for me to see what's underneath. Fear. Exhaustion. Maybe something more.

A breeze kicks up the dust around us. She brushes a strand of hair behind her ear, then finally meets my gaze. "I didn't expect to see you here."

"Same." I pause. "You running from something?"

She blinks. Too fast. Her mouth opens like she might deny it, but nothing comes out.

"Look," I say, backing off a step. "Whatever brought you here, maybe this isn't the place for it."

She flinches like I slapped her. Then the walls go back up. "Don't worry. I'm not staying."

She walks past me, stiff and unshakable. But the way her hands tremble as she reaches for her phone, that tells me everything I need to know.

Elena Dawson is in trouble.

Again.

And whether I like it or not, I still give a damn.

She's almost to the parking area when her phone buzzes.

I see the shift in her shoulders first, like someone just ran a cold knife down her spine. She doesn't unlock it. Just stares at the preview message: a symbol. One she clearly recognizes.

"Elena," I call out.

She doesn't turn. Doesn't move.

I take a few steps toward her, cautious, like she's a skittish colt about to bolt. "What is it?"

She finally looks back, eyes narrowed, lips parted like she wants to say something but can't get it out. Her hand clenches the phone tighter, knuckles white.

"It's nothing," she says, but her voice is brittle.

I don't buy it. "Right. Just another friendly message that turns your face that shade of pale?"

"Jack, don't."

"I'm not the one standing out here shaking."

That gets her. Her jaw tenses, but she lifts her chin like she's daring me to call her out again.

"You gonna tell me who sent that text?" I ask.

"I said drop it." Her voice cracks right at the end.

We stare at each other for a beat too long. Then, before I can press again, she turns back toward her SUV and climbs inside, slamming the door.

Through the windshield, I see her hands shaking on the steering wheel. Then she starts the engine and pulls away in a cloud of dust.

Whatever that message was, it rattled her to the core.

And I've got the sinking feeling that this wasn't just some awkward run-in at a county auction.

This is the beginning of something worse.

I stay rooted to the same spot long after the dust settles.

The voices of the auction crowd return to their usual rhythm, but I'm not listening. I'm staring at the spot where her taillights vanished down the gravel road, wondering why the hell my chest feels like it's stuck in a vise.

Something's off. More than off, it's sideways.

And now it's clawing at me.

I run a hand down my face, frustration simmering just below the surface. I'd finally gotten to a place where I wasn't thinking about her. About him. About the wreckage they left behind.

And now? One look, one damn rescue, and I'm right back in the thick of it.

Tom appears beside me, the same steady presence he's been since Declan and I started this place, holding two paper cups of coffee. "Well," he says, passing one over. "That was dramatic."

I grunt. "You could say that."

He follows my gaze. "Was that Elena?"

I nod once.

"She looks rough." Tom sips his coffee, watching me. "You gonna pretend you don't care?"

I don't answer. Because pretending would be a lie. And I've done enough lying to myself to last a lifetime.

I glance down the road again, jaw tight. Whatever she's running from, I've got the sinking feeling it's coming here next.

Chapter 2

In the Shadows

ELENA

The glow of my phone screen is the only light in the room.

I'm curled up on the edge of my threadbare couch, knees tucked under my chin, heart pounding with every buzz, every ping, every vibration that rattles against the coffee table like a countdown. Three voicemails. Five texts. All unknown numbers. All vague, threatening, and anonymous.

"You should've left it buried."

"People are watching."

"Next time, we won't knock."

Each one colder than the last. Each one delivered with the kind of precision that makes my skin crawl.

I haven't slept in almost forty-eight hours. Not really. Just shallow dozing with one eye open and the front door double bolted. Even now, I keep glancing toward the windows, half-expecting to see shadows moving behind the thin, sagging curtains. It's irrational. Paranoid.

Except... maybe it's not.

My apartment used to be a safe place. Small but cozy. Now it feels like a box closing in. The wallpaper peels near the baseboards. The ticking of the old wall clock echoes like a hammer. Every creak from the hallway sends a jolt through my chest.

I press play on the most recent voicemail.

Static. Then a muffled voice, warped through a voice distorter. "He left you things. We want them back."

I delete it before it finishes, throat tight.

I hate that I still call this place home. I hate that after everything, burying a husband who wasn't who he claimed to be, after months of trying to outrun the guilt, I'm right back here. Trapped in this shoebox of a life with nothing but ghosts for company.

A loud thud from the alley below makes me jump. I fumble the phone, heart hammering, breath shallow. It's just a dumpster lid. Probably. Maybe. Doesn't matter. My hands are shaking again.

I glance toward the envelope on the kitchen counter, the one I told myself I wouldn't open. Again.

But I already know what's inside.

The letter. The one I found tucked inside the lining of his old jacket last week. I'd gone looking for a reason to hate him less. What I found was worse: a half-apology and a coded list of names and locations.

Dangerous names.

Ones I thought were gone forever.

I grip the throw pillow tighter, pulling it against my chest like a shield.

It's only a matter of time before someone comes looking for that letter. Or me. And I can't stay here, pretending I'm not one phone call away from falling apart.

I close my eyes and exhale slowly, steadying my pulse. There's only one person I can think of who might be able to help.

And he's the last man on Earth I want to ask.

Lisa's already waiting when I arrive at our usual booth, tucked in the back of Rose's Café like a quiet refuge. She's got her reading glasses perched on her head, a laptop open in front of her, and a cinnamon latte steaming by her elbow. One look at me and she closes the screen.

"You look like hell," she says softly, sliding the extra coffee she ordered across the table.

"I feel worse."

I wrap both hands around the cup, letting the heat sink into my frozen fingers. She doesn't push right away. Just watches me the way only Lisa can; gentle, concerned, and way too perceptive.

"Is it the messages again?"

I nod, throat too tight to speak.

Lisa sighs. "You need to go to someone. The police, maybe?"

"They won't do anything. I don't even know who I'm supposed to be afraid of."

She leans in. "Then go to Jack."

The name hits like a punch to the chest. I flinch, spilling a little coffee.

Lisa doesn't back down. "He was close to your husband. He has military training. He knows how to manage threats. If anyone can help you sort through this mess, it's him."

"I don't know if I can." I whisper, shaking my head. "He hates me."

"Because of what your husband did?"

"Because I didn't stop it. Because I was part of it... even if I didn't realize it until it was too late."

Her gaze softens. "You don't know that. Maybe Jack doesn't either."

I want to believe her. I really do. But all I can picture is the look in Jack's eyes when we locked gazes at the auction. Jack was wary, guarded, and perceivably angry. Like I was a ghost he hadn't finished burying.

"You don't have to trust him," Lisa says gently. "Just trust yourself enough to know when you need backup."

I sip the coffee, willing it to chase the chill out of my bones. It doesn't work.

But Lisa's words linger like the last light before dusk.

And I wonder if maybe, just maybe, I'm not as alone as I think.

I'm back home by late afternoon, the sky outside the windows already tinged with gray. Rain threatens at the edges, the kind that smells like metal and settles into your bones.

I pull the envelope from the kitchen counter with slow fingers. The paper worn, the seal already cracked from how many times I've opened and closed it. Inside is the letter I found, one I wish I'd never read, and one I can't seem to throw away.

The handwriting is unmistakable. Declan's.

My chest tightens as I unfold the page.

"El,

If you're reading this, something's gone wrong. I know I don't deserve your trust, but I need you to believe me when I say I didn't mean for it to end like this. The names enclosed... they're not what they seem. Some are enemies, some were friends. Keep this safe. Don't trust anyone. Not even..."

The ink smudges there. A coffee stain or maybe a tear. Maybe mine.

I pull out the list tucked behind the letter. Half-coded names, coordinates, phrases I don't recognize but know better than to dismiss. A few locations are circled, one of them close. Too close. One name stands out more than the others.

Jack Harrison.

I blink hard. My stomach twists.

What was Declan doing tracking Jack's movements? Was it paranoia? Or was it something worse?

There's a knock, sudden and loud, at the door.

I jump, papers fluttering from my hands like broken feathers.

Another knock. Louder.

I move to the peephole, breath held tight in my throat. But no one's there. Just the flickering hallway light and the sound of my pulse thudding in my ears.

I wait.

Nothing.

When I finally crack the door open, the hall is empty.

But taped to the outside of the doorframe, barely visible, is a small, folded piece of paper.

My name written on it. Just my first name. In red ink.

And I know, without opening it, that someone's watching.

And I am out of time.

My hands won't stop shaking as I pull it from the door.

I lock the door and shove the deadbolt into place, pressing my back against the frame as if it'll hold the weight of everything crashing in.

The note still sits on the counter. Unopened. But it might as well be screaming.

I don't need to read it. I already know what it says.

I'm being watched. All the tactical calm they drilled into me, it's gone.

I pace the living room, arms wrapped tight around myself. Every creak in the floorboards above, every whisper of wind against the window sends my nerves skittering.

I can't stay here. That much is clear.

Declan's voice echoes in my head, *"Don't trust anyone."* But he also wrote something else, didn't he? Something just before the ink blurred. *Not even...*

Not even who? Jack? Himself? I don't know. And that's the part that terrifies me most.

I slide open the drawer beside the couch and pull out the manila folder I'd hidden there weeks ago. Inside are the files Declan left behind. Bank records. Notes scribbled in code. A copy of the deed to some rural property I never knew he owned.

I throw it all into a bag, add the original letter and the red-inked note, and zip it shut. My keys are on the hook. My phone buzzes again. It's another unknown number. I silence it without looking.

At the door, I hesitate. Just for a second.

Then I whisper, "I have no choice."

And I step out into the night.

Rain begins to fall harder. Cold and needling drops that soak through my jacket before I make it to the car. I don't look back. I can't.

I start the engine.

Headlights flare behind me.

I check the mirror. A dark sedan sits half a block down, no lights, engine off. Too clean. Too still. My skin crawls.

I grip the steering wheel and hit the gas.

Jack Harrison's ranch isn't close; it's outside the city limits almost in the middle of nowhere.

I just pray I'm not already too late.

The windshield wipers thud a quick rhythm, barely keeping up with the sheets of rain blurring the road ahead. My fingers ache from gripping the wheel too tight, but I can't let up. Not until I'm sure I'm alone.

Every time I check the mirror, that same car is there. Not tailgating. Not passing. Just… there. Distant. Patient. Like they're waiting for something.

I don't know if it's paranoia or proof, and right now, it doesn't matter. Either one is reason enough to keep driving.

I take the long way out of town, twisting through side streets, doubling back, cutting through a gas station lot. But the car stays with me, always two turns behind, like a shadow that won't let go.

Finally, past the edge of the last subdivision, I floor it. My little SUV groans in protest, tires kicking up water as I barrel onto the county road that leads to Jack's property. Miles of fields stretch out on either side, dark and empty. I breathe for the first time in what feels like hours.

The sedan doesn't follow.

At least, not that I can see.

But I still don't feel safe.

The rain is still pouring down when I turn onto the gravel road that leads to the ranch. My headlights catch on the gate just ahead.

My pulse skips.

I park just outside the gate and kill the engine. For a moment, I just sit there in the silence, rain tapping against the roof, heart thudding like a warning.

What if he slams the door in my face?

What if he's part of this, and I'm walking into a trap?

I start the engine and make the turn onto the ranch Declan once called home. A place that, for a time, felt like it belonged to all three of us. But I haven't been back since Declan died.

The long driveway is familiar and foreign all at once. As I pass the first bend, I notice the changes; fences repaired and gates replaced. There are cattle now, scattered across the valley like quiet shadows. When I crest the last hill, the ranch house comes into view, its windows catching the headlights. Off in the distance, I spot the old barn, standing tall again. Jack must've salvaged it.

They had a dream once. And when Declan died, I thought it died with him. So I walked away. Left the pieces behind.

I park at the end of the new stone walkway Jack must have laid. The rain is steady now, tapping against the windshield in soft percussion. I turn off the engine, reach for the manila folder in the passenger seat, and hold it close; shielding it from the rain, but also cradling it like armor. It contains everything. And I'm not sure who it's protecting more; me, or the truth inside.

Then I step out of the car and make a run for the porch. Not sure if I am running for cover or from whoever had been following me. Maybe both.

Behind me, I hear the quiet click of a camera. A red light vanishes in the dark. Or maybe I imagined it.

The porch light flicks on just as I reach the front steps, and the door opens.

I freeze.

Jack's silhouette fills the doorway. He's tall, broad, and unmoving. His arms crossed, and even from this distance, I can see the tight set of his jaw. He hasn't changed a bit. Maybe a little more weathered, maybe more guarded. But the same intensity is there, radiating from him like heat from wildfire.

My feet feel like they're made of stone, but I make myself take the last few steps to the door.

He doesn't open it. Doesn't move. Just waits.

"I need your help," I say before he can speak. My voice cracks, and I hate how raw it sounds.

Jack's eyes drop to the folder clutched to my chest, then flick back to my face. "You showing up here in the middle of the night with that look in your eyes says a whole lot more than you just did."

I open my mouth to respond, but he finally shifts, stepping aside and pulling the door wider.

"You're soaked. Get in before you start shivering on my porch."

Relief floods through me, but I try not to show it. I nod once and step inside.

The smell of woodsmoke, coffee, and something faintly herbal hit me instantly, warming me just from the aroma. I haven't been here in years, but the smell is still the same. I try not to look around too much. Too many memories I'm still not ready to face.

Jack shuts the door behind me, slow and deliberate. "You want to tell me what's going on?"

I swallow hard, suddenly hyper-aware of the mud on my boots, the damp hair clinging to my face. "Not yet. But I will."

He studies me for a long moment, then nods once. "You look like hell."

I huff a quiet laugh. "You don't look so great yourself."

For a second, something passes between us. Not forgiveness. Not even understanding. But something old and tired and unfinished.

Jack gestures toward the couch. "Take your coat off. Sit. You can start talking when you're ready."

I nod again and ease down onto the familiar leather cushions, clutching the folder tighter.

For the first time in days, the noise in my head dims.

And I realize I might finally be somewhere safe.

Maybe.

Chapter 3

Things Unsaid

JACK

She's standing on my porch like she owns the place, and like it's the last place on earth she wants to be.

Elena Dawson. Or at least, that's the name I knew her by when she married Declan. Before the secrets. Before the classified past I only started to suspect.

I grip the doorframe, fighting the instinct to close it again. She looks soaked and road-weary, her clothes clinging to her, hair dripping like she's walked through a storm just to find me.

Which, knowing her, might not be far from the truth.

"You're soaked. Get in before you start shivering on my porch," I tell her, because it's easier than asking the hundred questions crowding my brain.

She hesitates for half a second, then steps over the threshold. Eyes avoiding me. Or maybe just the memories.

I can't help but watch her. Not the way I used to, back when things were simple. No, now I watch her like I'm waiting for her to crack. Because there's something brittle in her movements. Something careful and rehearsed. Like she's holding herself together with sheer will.

"I didn't expect company tonight," I say, shutting the door behind her.

She drops her bag by the door and pushes damp hair out of her face. "Wasn't planning to be company."

"Still managed it," I mutter.

That earns me a flick of her eyebrow. "You going to glare at me all night, or is there a towel somewhere in this charming fortress?"

I grunt and nod toward the hall. "Linen closet. Second door on the left."

She disappears down the hallway, and I finally exhale.

It's been years since she's been in this house. Years since Declan brought her around, bright-eyed and full of secrets. Now she's back, shadowed and soaked to the bone, clutching a folder like it holds her last ounce of safety.

And I can't shake the feeling that trouble just walked through my front door.

She returns a minute later, an old flannel towel draped over her shoulders. Still somehow managing to wear it like armor.

I clear my throat. "You hungry?"

She lifts one shoulder. "Depends. You still burn everything you touch?"

My lips twitch despite myself. "I've improved. Slightly."

There it is. That old spark of hers. The sass that used to drive me insane. The same spark I thought I was immune to now.

I head to the kitchen and grab leftovers from the fridge; roast chicken, cold cornbread, something that might've been green beans once. I plate two servings in silence.

When I glance over, she's already seated at the table. Looking too calm. Too polite.

It's a performance. I've seen her real fear. And it's never this quiet.

This woman is scared.

And I want to know why.

We eat in silence at first.

The kind that hums just under the skin. The silence is too loud to ignore, but too tight to relax. Her fork scrapes lightly against the plate, and she takes small, methodical bites, like chewing is the only thing keeping her from unraveling.

"Still think I burn everything?" I ask, nodding to her half-empty plate.

She swallows and lifts her brows. "Let's just say it's edible. That's progress."

I snort and take another bite of cornbread. Dry. Could've used more butter. But she's eating, and that tells me more than her words do.

"You've lost weight," I say before I can stop myself.

She stiffens, the fork hovering midair. "Observant as ever."

"I'm not trying to insult you."

"You're doing a great job anyway."

The tension snaps between us like an old rope, frayed yet familiar.

I sigh and lean back in my chair, arms crossing. "You gonna tell me what's really going on?"

She's toying with a green bean that's long past its prime. "Not yet."

"Then why are you here?"

That gets her. Her eyes flick to mine, sharp and tired. "Because I didn't know where else to go."

The words hit harder than I expect. Raw. Unscripted. Honest in a way that feels like a bruise.

She pushes her plate away and leans back. "I know what you think of me. I know you think I was part of whatever Declan got caught up in."

I study her, noting the twitch of her fingers, the way she presses her lips together too tightly. She's bracing for a fight I'm not sure I want to give.

"What I think," I say slowly, "is that you showed up here with a folder you haven't let out of your grip, and you're looking over your shoulder like the devil's on your heels. That tells me something's wrong."

"It is."

The words are a whisper, barely there. And the vulnerability in them punches a hole through every defense I've tried to rebuild.

"I'll tell you," she says after a long pause, "but not tonight. Not yet."

"Fine." I get up and start clearing the plates. "But if you're going to stay here, you need to stop treating me like the enemy."

"I'm not sure who my enemies are anymore."

That quiet admission stops me cold.

And suddenly, I'm not as sure of things as I was an hour ago either.

The knock comes just as I'm drying the last plate.

Not loud. Just two calm, deliberate raps. Enough to set my spine straight.

Elena goes rigid. Her hand flies to the folder again like she thinks it'll disappear if she holds it tight enough.

I set the dish towel down and grab the bat I keep leaning by the door. Old habit. Hard to break. Especially this time of night.

"Expecting someone?" I ask, low.

She shakes her head, eyes wide. "No one knows I'm here."

I open the door slowly, ready for a fight.

Instead, there's a man in a dark coat standing on the porch. Clean-cut, mid-thirties, holding an envelope in one gloved hand. He doesn't flinch at the sight of me, just looks me up and down like he's assessing a tool.

"Jack Harrison?"

Sam Carlisle.

He knows damn well who I am. We spent enough years stacked shoulder to shoulder in the worst corners of the world.

The fact that he's using my full name, like I'm some stranger, tells me this isn't just a visit.

He's not talking to me.

He's making sure *she* doesn't ask too many questions. Not yet.

He tilts his head. "I need a word. About Declan."

The name hits like a brick to the sternum.

Behind me, I hear the creak of the floorboards. Elena steps into view, and the man's eyes shift to her instantly.

"Elena," he says with a polite nod. "You look… well."

She doesn't answer. Her hand tightens around the folder. "Who are you?"

"Call me Sam," he says simply, then holds out the envelope. "I have something you need to see. I'm a friend of Declan's."

"Declan didn't have friends," I snap.

Sam doesn't react. "He had people he trusted. Sometimes that's not the same thing."

Elena steps forward and takes the envelope with careful fingers. She doesn't open it right away.

"What's in it?" I ask.

"Information. Proof. Names. You'll want to read it. But more importantly, you need to understand that what's coming isn't random."

"Then tell us who sent you."

Sam's smile doesn't reach his eyes. "I'm not at liberty to say."

Convenient.

I step between him and Elena. "You show up at my door, mention a dead man, and refuse to say who sent you. That's not how trust works."

Sam nods once, like he expected that. "I don't need you to trust me. Just… read the contents. Carefully."

He turns to go.

But before he steps off the porch, he looks back at Elena.

"They know you're here," he says softly. "You don't have much time. Get her a new phone Jack, hers has been compromised."

The sound of his footsteps fades quickly into the rain. No car starts. No headlights appear. Just wet silence pressing in around us.

Elena stares at the envelope like it might catch fire.

And I can't shake the feeling that whatever just landed in our laps, it's only the beginning.

I shut the door behind Sam, double-checking the lock before I turn back around.

Elena hasn't moved. Still clutching the envelope, still staring at the spot where Sam stood.

"Elena, give me your phone."

She hands me her phone with no hesitation. I drop the phone to the floor, stepping on it with my boot, incapacitating it before tossing it into the fireplace. It crackles and smells up the room, but at least it's destroyed.

"You okay?" I ask.

She doesn't answer, just swallows hard and moves to the couch like she's sleepwalking. I follow, keeping a cautious distance. She sits, lays the envelope across her lap, and slowly peels it open.

Inside is a single folded map, worn soft along the creases. She opens it and lays it across the coffee table, smoothing it with shaking hands. It's a standard highway map of the western counties, until she flips it over.

On the back, drawn in heavy black ink, is a symbol. A jagged half-circle with a line through it, slashed like a crescent moon caught mid-fall.

Elena lets out a slow, brittle breath. Her fingers hover over it, but she doesn't touch.

I lean closer. "What is that?"

Her voice is barely above a whisper. "Declan used to mark his files with this when something was dangerous. Off-limits. He said if I ever saw it outside his notes… it meant someone else had gotten too close."

A chill moves across the back of my neck.

There's a location marked, and just north of it, a small, smudged dot near my property line.

She hesitates. "Declan marked you too. I think he was tracking you. Or someone was."

It hits low and cold, that realization. Not just being drawn into this, but already being in it, maybe long before I knew.

She points again. "That other mark... it's where we camped. Before everything went sideways.""

I study her profile. Elena's jaw is tense, her eyes darting, and her thin fingers now gripping the map like a lifeline.

"You recognize it?" I ask.

She nods. "It was a backup site. Declan's contingency plan, he called it. I thought it was just one of his weird security obsessions. But this…" Her voice trails off.

"This means someone else knows," I finish for her.

She meets my gaze. "And if Sam's telling the truth, that someone is watching us. Watching me."

Silence thickens between us, filled with unspoken memories and too many regrets.

After looking at the map a few minutes longer, she folds the map and tucks it back into the envelope like it might bite her. "I didn't want to drag you into this."

I sit beside her, not close, but close enough. "You didn't. I opened the door." Doesn't mean I didn't hesitate. Doesn't mean I'm not wondering if I'll regret it. But there's no going back now.

Her lips twitch like she wants to argue. But she doesn't. She just leans back against the couch, eyes heavy with fear she won't say out loud.

And I know one thing for sure, whoever's coming for her...

They'll have to go through me first

Chapter 4

Ranch Duty

ELENA

The rain hasn't let up.

It drums against the tin roof like a warning, relentless and cold. I watch it streak the kitchen window as I sip the last of my lukewarm coffee. Jack sits across from me at the small wooden table, flipping through a weather report on his phone like it might magically change. It won't.

"Looks like you're stuck here for a while," he mutters, not looking up.

"Great," I say, too quickly. My voice flattens under the weight of my own sarcasm. "Just what every woman dreams of; being marooned in the middle of nowhere with a man who barely tolerates her."

His eyes flick to mine, unreadable. "I wouldn't go that far."

I raise a brow. "Which part?"

Jack leans back in his chair, arms crossed. "The barely part."

It's so absurd, so gruff and dry, and pure Jack, I let out a soft laugh before I can stop myself. His mouth twitches, just slightly. Almost a smile. Almost.

Outside, thunder rumbles low, and the lights flicker once. I stare at the overhead bulb like it might blink out for good. Jack follows my gaze.

"You afraid of storms now?"

"I'm not afraid," I lie. "Just not a fan of being trapped."

He nods like he understands. Maybe he does. We both know a thing or two about being cornered.

"I've got extra blankets in the linen closet," he says. "And Declan's room has still got heat. If the power goes, there's a backup generator wired to the main."

"You always this prepared?"

He shrugs. "Comes with the territory."

Another roll of thunder shakes the windows. I press my palm to the table, grounding myself.

Silence stretches between us. Not quite comfortable. Not quite hostile. Just… unsteady. Like standing on an old rope bridge. Just one wrong word and it all goes crashing down.

"I can help around here," I say suddenly. "While I'm stuck."

Jack lifts his brow. "You offering to do chores?"

"I'm not useless."

"Didn't say you were."

I glare at him. "I can handle more than you think."

His jaw flexes, but he doesn't argue. Just gives a slow, measured nod. "All right. We'll see."

It's not a truce. Not even close. But for the first time, it doesn't feel like we're enemies, either.

Just two people caught in a storm.

Waiting to see which one of us cracks first.

Jack gives me Declan and I's old room for the night. It's small, barely enough room for the bed and dresser, but it smells like cedar and clean cotton sheets, and maybe a hint of the man who once slept here. After the last few nights sleeping with one eye open and a knife under my pillow, this feels like a luxury suite.

Jack knocked lightly before I turned in, holding out an old pair of sweats and a faded T-shirt. "Figured you didn't come with pajamas," he said. I took them without arguing.

I sit on the edge of the bed for a long time before lying down. The rain batters the window like it's trying to get in. But the walls here feel thick. Safe. Solid in a way I haven't felt in months.

For once, sleep comes easy.

When I wake, pale morning light filters through the curtain and the storm is still going strong. It may even be worse than before. The windowpane streaked with water; the wind whistled through the cracks in the old frame. Somewhere in the house, wood groans, and I swear I hear Jack mutter a curse under his breath.

I sit up slowly, the borrowed clothes twisted around me. As I swing my legs off the bed, I catch my reflection in the mirror on the dresser. The shirt hangs loosely on my frame, I have lost weight. My eyes are still puffy with sleep, but it's the logo on the shirt that stops me.

The fabric is soft from years of wear, the emblem faded but unmistakable; an old unit insignia from Jack and Declan's time in the military. A circular patch with a phoenix holding lightning and an arrow, stitched above a cracked motto I never bothered to learn.

I swallow hard, fingers brushing over the image like it might answer all the questions I've been too afraid to ask.

Why did Jack keep this? Why give it to me?

A lump forms in my throat, but I push it down. I'm too tired for more ghosts. Not this morning.

I gather myself and finally make my way to the kitchen.

Jack's already there, coffee mug in hand, the scent sharp and grounding. He looks like he hasn't slept, but he nods toward the pot. "Help yourself."

I pour a cup and warm my hands around it before sitting across from him at the table. The silence is companionable this time, not tense. Maybe because it's early. Maybe because neither of us has enough energy to pick a fight yet.

"I meant what I said last night," I murmur. "About helping."

He eyes me over the rim of his mug. "You sure?"

"I can shovel a stall."

He sets his cup down with a quiet thunk. "Then grab boots and don't expect a gold star. Ranch work doesn't care if you're having a bad day."

"Boots? I didn't really come prepared, Jack."

He eyes me with something I can't quite put my finger on, "When you disappeared after Declan's death, I boxed up some things you left around the house. It's been a few years, but I think I remember putting your old boots in that box."

I smile faintly, surprised by the gesture, but also by how right that feels.

The barn smells like damp hay and old wood. It creaks and groans under the weight of the storm, but it's dry inside, and for now, that's enough.

Jack hands me a pitchfork without a word. I take it, trying to ignore the way his gaze lingers a beat too long, like he's waiting for me to fumble it.

I don't.

We work in a rhythm that's more tolerable than I expect. Jack feeding the horses, me forking fresh straw into stalls. The rain is a steady background drumbeat, loud but comforting.

It's the silence between us that feels louder.

At one point, I reach to brush my hair behind my ear and wince slightly, rubbing my wrist. It's nothing, just a dull ache, an old training injury flaring up when I overdo it.

But when I glance up, Jack is watching.

He doesn't say anything. Just shifts his attention back to the hay bale he's dragging. Still, I feel his gaze like a spotlight.

He noticed. Of course he did.

We work a while longer in near-silence. It's not unpleasant, exactly. Just... charged. I don't know if it's the storm or the tension or something else rising between us like heat off the floor.

Later, I retreat to the loft, climbing the ladder with muscle memory from a life that feels like someone else's. I used to do this kind of work with Declan and Jack. Before everything cracked.

The loft is quiet and warm. I tuck into a hay filled corner with my knees pulled up and lean my head back against the barn wall.

My fingers find the locket beneath my shirt before I realize what I'm doing. It's small, old, and dented, but it was an anniversary gift from Declan, back when we still believed in promises. I flip it open, thumb grazing the photo inside. The two of us on a summer day, grinning like fools; I remember it well.

I don't even realize I'm crying until a tear hits the back of my hand.

I wipe it away quickly, but it's too late. Footsteps creak below. Jack pauses at the base of the ladder. He doesn't climb. Doesn't say a word. Just lingers.

Then, just as quietly as he came, he walks away.

I exhale slowly, pressing the locket to my chest.

Somehow, that silent moment, unspoken and raw, feels more intimate than anything we've said all day.

Eventually, the quiet becomes too much. I climb down and slip back into the house, drawn by the smell of coffee and something heavier: unfinished business.

Later, I'm sorting through a box Jack left on the dining room table, it's water-stained and full of Declan's old paperwork. The kind of mess no one really wants to deal with: receipts, scribbled notes, faded maps, forms yellowed at the edges.

I told him I didn't need any more pieces of Declan.

But I couldn't stop myself from opening it.

The rain still hasn't let up. The sound of it has faded into background noise, like a heartbeat I can't quite ignore. I dig deeper into the box, past an old pocketknife and photos I don't want to look at.

Then I see it: a small black ledger.

It's worn at the edges, bound in cracked leather. I hesitate for half a second, then flip it open.

At first, it looks like nonsense. Columns of numbers, dates, initials. But as I scan the pages, my stomach drops.

The dates.

I recognize them.

They match the entries from Declan's letter. From the names and locations he warned me about. Each one linked to some shadowy operation he never wanted written down. And here they are, coded in his handwriting.

One name is circled. Bold red ink, like a warning: M. Thorne.

Thorne. The name stops me cold. It's familiar, but I can't place it. Not yet. And that makes it worse.

My blood runs cold.

I grip the table edge to steady myself. The room feels too small, the walls too close.

I don't know who M. Thorne is, but Declan circled that name like it meant the end of everything.

And now I'm here, standing in Jack's kitchen, holding a key to something bigger than either of us realized.

Whatever this is, it didn't die with Declan.

It just started breathing again.

I close the ledger slowly, like shutting it too hard might wake the ghosts inside. My hands are still trembling, but I tuck it back into the box and slide the lid closed. Out of sight, but definitely not out of mind.

Jack hasn't said a word since I started going through it. He's across the room now, oiling the hinges on the back door with that same focused silence he uses like a shield. I watch him for a second too long.

He doesn't glance up, but I know he feels it. That weight in the air between us that wasn't there before.

"You always this quiet when someone's world starts unraveling in your kitchen?" I ask.

He straightens, wipes his hands on a rag. "You looked like you needed space."

"I need a hell of a lot more than that."

He crosses the room slowly. Not threatening. Not cautious either. Just steady. Like he's done this before; navigated grief with his boots still muddy.

"You want to talk about what you found?"

I shake my head. "Not yet. I'm still trying to convince myself it's real."

Jack leans against the counter, arms crossed. "It's real. I've seen that look before."

"What look?"

"The one where the floor drops out, and you realize you've been standing on a lie."

That catches me off guard.

For a moment, we just breathe. The storm outside seems quieter, like it's listening too.

"I don't know who to trust," I admit. "Not even Declan, not anymore."

"You trusted him once."

"Yeah. And look where that got me."

I meet Jack's eyes then, really meet them. And what I see there isn't judgment. It's something else. Understanding, maybe. Or its bruised cousin.

"You trusted him too," I say quietly.

He doesn't deny it. "He was my partner, and my best friend since we were kids. You know I trusted him with my life."

The space between us shrinks, not physically, but in the way two people stop pretending they're on opposite sides of something.

"Thanks for not making me leave," I say.

He nods. "And here I thought you might burn the place down first."

A half-smile tugs at my lips.

Whatever this thing is between us, it's shifting.

Not fixed. Not forgiven.

But maybe… just maybe… no longer broken.

Chapter 5

Between the Lines

JACK

The storm's almost passed, but the ranch house still feels full of pressure. Like the house is holding its breath, waiting for the next blow. I stand at the kitchen sink, staring out at the pasture where mist clings low to the ground, the cattle barely rising above it. The land's quiet now, soaked through, a patchwork of mud and memory.

I can't stop thinking about Declan.

He was my friend, and brother, in every way that mattered. We served together, bled together, buried things overseas that we never spoke of again. Then, back home, we tried to build something real. This ranch, our partnership: it had been a dream since we were kids.

And then, just like that, he changed.

Pulled away. Grew distant. Cold. Like I'd done something unforgivable that he wouldn't name.

I remember our last argument like it just happened. Voices raised in the barn, his jaw tight, my fists clenched. He accused me of not understanding. I accused him of running. We never found middle ground.

The worst part? I still don't know if I lost him to something external, or if I missed something right in front of me. Did I break something? Was it my failure?

A soft sound behind me pulls me out of the spiral.

Elena.

She's quiet as she enters the kitchen, barefoot in my old T-shirt and sweats. My unit insignia sits faded across her chest, and it twists something low in my gut.

That shirt used to mean something. The insignia wasn't just mine. It was ours, Declan's and mine, and so many others. And now she's wearing it like a wound she never asked for but refuses to hide.

Seeing it on her, it shouldn't matter.

But it does.

She pours herself a cup of coffee and joins me at the table without asking. Like this has always been her place. Like we aren't standing in the shadow of the same man.

I clear my throat. "You ever see Declan change?"

She stiffens slightly. Doesn't answer right away.

"I mean really change," I press. "Not just getting quiet. I'm talking full personality shift. Secrets. Distance."

Her fingers tighten around the mug.

"Yeah," she says finally. "Right before he died. He started locking drawers. Erasing messages. Looking over his shoulder like someone was following him."

I nod slowly. "He said something to me during our last fight. Something I didn't understand at the time. Told me I'd be safer if I kept my head down."

Elena sets her coffee down, her jaw working like she's chewing something bitter. "He told me that too. Almost word for word."

We sit in silence, the weight of it pressing down.

I look at her. "I don't know if I failed him... or if he failed me first."

She meets my gaze. And for the first time since she showed up on my porch, she doesn't look like she's trying to run.

"We both deserve the truth," she says quietly.

And I realize we're not just haunted by the same ghost. No, we're trying to fight our way out of the same fog.

She disappears down the hall and returns a few minutes later holding the manila folder I first saw clutched to her chest when she arrived. She sets it gently on the table between us, like it might break.

"I didn't show you this before," she says, her voice quiet but steady, "because I wasn't sure I could trust you with it. Or myself."

I nod once, giving her space.

She opens the manilla envelope and pulls out a series of printed documents, some official, others clearly personal. Notes scribbled in the margins. Dates. Coordinates. Names I don't recognize, highlighted and circled. There's a rhythm to it, a pattern hiding in plain sight.

"This is what Declan left behind," she says. "What I've been piecing together from his things. He was tracking something or someone. I think it started years ago, maybe while you two were still overseas."

I scan the first sheet. Something about the formatting rings familiar. Intel brief summaries. Not military issue, but close. Like someone was mimicking the style without authorization.

"Who else saw this?" I ask.

"No one," she says. "Only me. And now you."

I catch a name halfway down the list and freeze.

"Elena," I say slowly, tapping the page. "This one, Isaac Voss. He was flagged on a watchlist we shared with intel teams overseas. Small-time smuggler turned private contractor. Dangerous. Unreliable."

Her eyes widen. "Declan met with him. There's a record of it. Denver, the spring before he died."

I look up. "That was around the time he stopped speaking to me."

We both sit back, tension winding tight again.

"I think we were pawns," she says, her voice low. "Declan got too close to something and didn't know how to protect us both."

I rub the back of my neck. "Or maybe he thought by cutting us out, he was keeping us safe."

She looks at me. "And instead, we're left holding the mess."

I study the table between us; papers, names, timelines, and shadows of a man we both thought we knew.

It's starting to come together.

And it's not good.

We work all afternoon reviewing the evidence that Declan had left us. The documents spread across the table like a battlefield map.

Elena kneels on one end, sorting papers by category; dates, contacts, and locations. I take the other, trying to string together connections from the mess Declan left behind. The storm outside has finally quieted, but the air between us crackles with the static of everything we don't yet know.

She passes me a page, then another. "Some of this is in Declan's handwriting. But these forms?" She lifts a stapled packet from the manila folder, brows drawing together. "These were taken from somewhere official. Internal."

I scan the document. It's routing slips, supply codes, signatures blacked out with thick ink. But not all of them. There, faint but visible in the corner: a clearance stamp and a designation I've seen before.

"Look at this," I say, tapping the margin. "This operation near El Paso… Voss was tied to it. And this supply route through Oklahoma? That's not military sanctioned. It's private."

She flips to another sheet, her voice low. "Voss. Thorne. These aren't low-level guys. And Declan wasn't just stumbling onto this. Declan was building something. A case. Quietly. And this envelope?" She holds it up like it weighs more now. "It wasn't just a warning."

I nod, scanning the margins again. "No. It's evidence. He marked these operations with initials: M.T., A.J., T-6. It's a pattern. These aren't random."

"T-6 we've seen before," Elena says. "But M.T. and A.J.... Declan must've known who they were. Or what role they played."

I lean back, pulse rising. "He didn't trust them enough to write their names. Just enough to track them."

She meets my eyes. "Then that's what we do now. We track them."

I nod slowly, brain working the angles. "T-6 could be Thorne. Or someone using his name. Could even be a unit designation. But if it's both?" I glance at her. "That's worse."

"Declan was in way over his head."

The conversation quiets for a beat. I glance at her, surprised by the focus in her expression. She's sharp. Determined. There's a steel under the surface I hadn't seen clearly until now.

"You're good at this," I say, almost without meaning to.

She looks up, surprised. "What?"

"This kind of work. Putting puzzles together."

She shrugs. "Military intel cross-training. And a lot of late nights trying not to fall apart."

Something in my chest shifts. Not quite sympathy. Not pity. Something closer to respect.

We keep working, side by side, as the hours bleed later into the evening. The room feels warmer. The distance between us smaller.

She taps a corner of one document. "This is all still just a theory, you know. A bunch of dots we haven't connected yet."

"Yeah," I say, eyes still scanning. "But it's more than we had yesterday."

Her lips curve. It's not a smile exactly, but something close.

Then she freezes.

"There's one more name," she says slowly. "I was saving it because I needed to be sure. I just... I think you'll recognize it."

Chapter 6

In the Dark

JACK

The power cuts without warning, plunging the house into silence.

I don't reach for the flashlight. A man trained for combat doesn't light up his position during a blackout. My eyes adjust quickly as I move toward the front door by memory, boots quiet against the wood floor.

Outside, gravel crunches, closer this time. Tires, not boots. A vehicle idles near the fence line, lights off. I duck below the window, careful not to silhouette myself. A dark SUV tucked where the trees meet open pasture.

"Elena," I call quietly. "Away from the windows."

No answer.

"Elena."

She appears in the doorway, manila folder clutched to her chest like it might stop a bullet. Her eyes are alert. Ready.

"I heard it too," she says.

I don't waste time. I move to the false panel behind the coat rack and pull the rifle free. Everything's right where I left it: blades, ammo, Glock. My hands move fast. Familiar. Anchored.

"If it was a friend, they'd have knocked," I say.

She nods, fear sharpening into something harder.

"There's a Glock in the pantry," I tell her. "False bottom under the lower shelf. Grab it. Extra mag's beside it."

Her eyes meet mine, steady. "You think I'll need it?"

"If I didn't, I wouldn't have told you where it was."

She hesitates. "Jack…"

"Don't open the door unless I call your full name."

"Elena Dawson. Got it."

She's gone in a blink. Quick. Focused. No wasted movement. Whoever trained her did a good job.

Another noise outside. I move through the dark toward the back of the house. Lightless. Silent.

Just in time to catch movement at the edge of the yard.

Not one figure. Two.

We're being surrounded.

I raise the rifle, pulse steady.

Whatever comes through that door, it's not walking out again if it means her harm.

I flatten myself against the wall, every sense on high alert. The cold of the rifle stock is grounding, a familiar weight against my shoulder. My breathing slows. I scan for details; movement, sounds, any indication of how many and how close.

A glimmer of motion near the tool shed. Another shape closer to the barn. Too practiced. These aren't amateurs. Whoever they are, they know how to move quiet.

I adjust my grip and move low along the interior wall, listening. The front porch creaks, just slightly. They're testing the perimeter.

I count seconds in my head, gauging the rhythm of their approach. Steady. Controlled. No panic. They're confident. That makes them dangerous.

Footsteps near the front door pause. One set. Then a soft click. Tools. Trying the lock.

I slip into position behind the old hutch angled near the entry, crouched low. The angle gives me a clear shot if the door opens.

A beat passes.

Then the sound of retreating steps. Whoever it was didn't like what they found. Or didn't find what they expected.

Behind me, a floorboard groans.

I twist, ready, but it's only Elena. She's crouched halfway down the hall, gun drawn, eyes wide but steady.

I shake my head, motioning her back. She doesn't move. Of course she doesn't.

I move to her, crouch beside her, voice a low whisper. "Two out back. One just tried the front. You see anything else?"

She nods toward the kitchen window. "There was one more, near the propane tank. Standing guard."

"Four," I mutter. "Too many for a coincidence."

"We're not making it through the night without a plan."

"I'm working on it."

She presses her lips together. "What do you need from me?"

Her steadiness surprises me. She's scared and I can see it, but she's holding it together with a soldier's discipline. And in this moment, she's not a widow or a liability.

She's my partner.

I meet her eyes. "You got my back?"

She doesn't blink. "Always."

Somewhere outside, a dog barks. Then silence again.

The storm may have passed, but something far worse is settling in.

And we're right in the middle of it.

We move like we've done this before, silent and practiced. A step at a time through the darkened hall, keeping low, communicating with nods and the flex of fingers.

I check the back windows first. One of the figures is pacing slow near the barn, head down, likely on comms. The other's vanished, but I can feel him out there, watching.

Elena follows close, her Glock held steady in a two-handed grip. I catch her checking corners instinctively, eyes sharp. For a second, it's like I'm on patrol again, with someone who knows how to survive.

We reach the den. I slip behind the window curtain just enough to watch the side yard. Nothing yet.

Then there's movement. One of them approaches the house from the east, crouched low, trying to keep his steps muffled on the wet grass.

"They're closing in," I murmur.

Elena edges beside me. "They're not casing anymore. They're preparing."

I nod. "Whatever they're after, they're willing to push for it tonight."

She looks toward the hallway. "We need to move. We can't defend from inside."

"I know."

We're already thinking the same thing. The house is too big to guard every entrance, too small to retreat inside if they force a breach. We'll need cover. High ground. And a fallback.

I glance at the firewood stack near the kitchen door. Concealed behind it, the storm cellar hatch is still dry. Sealed. A good fallback point if we're outgunned.

"Go to the kitchen," I whisper. "See if you can spot the one near the propane tank again. If he's moving, I want to know his direction."

She hesitates, just a beat. Then nods and slips away like smoke.

I shift my position back toward the entryway, heart pounding a steady rhythm. I don't feel fear. Not exactly. It's more like an edge sharpening inside me.

We've got four trained intruders on the perimeter.

We've got no power and no backup.

But I've got Elena.

And for the first time in a long time, I'm not fighting alone.

The house has settled into an unnatural stillness. Even the creak of the walls in the wind has gone quiet, like the building itself is listening.

I crouch beside the window again, scanning. Nothing new. Whoever they are, they're smart. Patient. That's what worries me. They're not amateurs looking for a quick break-in. No, they're staging.

My gaze tracks to the tree line. Still. Too still.

"Elena," I whisper.

She's back before I even finish the thought, sliding into place beside me with her shoulders low and breath steady.

"He moved west," she murmurs. "Toward the generator housing."

"Then he's not just waiting. He's checking infrastructure."

She nods. "They're going to cut off every option we have."

Not if we take the initiative.

I press my back to the wall and think fast. The storm cellar's still our best fallback. It's concealed beneath the stacked firewood near the kitchen door, sealed with a reinforced hatch that blends into the porch decking. Declan and I built it to withstand worse than storms. Most wouldn't even notice it unless they were looking. But we need to buy time, divide their attention.

"Elena, listen carefully. There's a trail. It's narrow and overgrown, off the east fence line. It leads to a dry creek bed about fifty yards out. There's a rusted shed down there I used for equipment staging a few years back."

She frowns. "You want me to run?"

"No. I want you to circle and distract. Fire a warning shot. Draw two of them away. Then fall back to the cellar."

She studies me like she's weighing whether I'm giving her a suicide mission. "And you?"

"I'll handle the other two."

Her jaw tightens. "Jack..."

"You said you've got my back," I say, quiet but firm.

"I do. That's why I'm saying we do this together."

"We are. Just on different ends."

For a long second, we stare at each other. The moment stretches, silent and taut. Then she nods and starts checking her mag. She lifts her arms to quickly twist her long hair into a low braid, securing it with a tie she pulls from her wrist. A movement that's practiced and efficient. No shine, no distraction. Just readiness.

"You better come out of this in one piece," she mutters.

"You too."

We split. Moving like silent shadows in opposite directions. No more words. Just the unspoken promise that whatever comes next, we're not backing down.

The trap is set.

Now it's just a matter of who steps into it first.

Chapter 7

Old Habits Die Hard

ELENA

The night air slices through my lungs like glass as I move along the east fence line, boots silent on the wet earth. The braid at the base of my neck sticks to the back of my shirt, damp with sweat and mist. I keep low, Glock secure in my grip, my thoughts a sharp whisper in the dark.

I know how to do this. I've done it before, in places much worse than this. The uniform didn't stay on long, but the training stuck, and so did the instincts.

The trail's narrower than Jack described it. Weeds claw at my pants, burrs catching on fabric as I duck beneath a split-rail post and slide behind a fallen cedar. The rusted shed looms ahead, still mostly intact. It's a ghost of utility, half-collapsed, but it'll do for cover.

I press my back to the wall and exhale slowly.

Focus.

Jack's out there, somewhere on the opposite side of the house, walking into the teeth of the threat. My job is to pull some of them away. Give him an opening. Maybe make them question how many people they're actually up against.

I raise the Glock and fire once, deliberately into the sky.

Then I wait.

It doesn't take long. Noise echoes faintly from the trees. Two shadows break off, jogging in my direction.

Got you.

I slip farther behind the shed, keeping low. My heart slams in my chest, adrenaline thundering through me, but my hands are steady. I scan the trees, counting my breaths.

Three.

Two.

One.

They arrive. Silent and tactical with their rifles drawn. I catch their silhouettes between the trees, flanking. Professional.

One of them signals. The other sweeps wide, heading toward the structure.

I backtrack two steps, silent. My heel brushes a loose board. It creaks.

He stops.

Listens.

And then he turns sharply, weapon raised.

I drop low, knees in the mud, heart pounding so loud I swear he can hear it. But he doesn't fire. He steps closer instead.

Ten feet.

Eight.

I steady my aim. I don't want to kill him, but I won't hesitate.

His radio crackles.

"North side breach. Possible entry."

The man stiffens, curses under his breath, and turns.

Jack.

He's making his move.

I stay low as they peel away, shadows slipping back into the dark.

One glance at the trees tells me everything I need to know.

They're falling for it.

Which means I need to move.

Fast.

JACK

The second Elena's shot cracks through the air, I move.

Low. Fast. Silent.

I circle wide around the porch, cutting through the shadows between the barn and the propane tank. Their attention's fractured. That is exactly what I hoped for. The two who headed east are out of my path. That leaves two. Maybe three if they brought backup.

But I don't hear movement from the back anymore. Just shallow breathing, too close to be mine.

I pause behind the rain barrel near the back corner of the house. From here, I've got a view of the back entrance. I can see dim outlines, moonlight stretching just enough to illuminate what I need. One figure. Close. Watching the house. He's waiting for a signal.

I shift to the left and grip the hilt of the blade in my boot. The rifle's ready, but a shot this close would draw the others. I need quiet.

I slip out and move fast.

The man turns a half-second too late.

I hit him low, knocking him off balance before he can shout. We struggle in the mud, boots scraping, arms tangled. He's strong, but I've got leverage, and years of instinct sharpened by memory. My knee drives into his ribs. He grunts, barely, but it's enough. I clamp a hand over his mouth and press the blade to his neck.

His body goes still.

"You blink wrong, I end you," I growl low against his ear. "Understand?"

A single, jerky nod.

Then I move. It's quick and clean. I drive the heel of my palm into the base of his skull, just below the occipital ridge. It's a move they drilled into us: fast, quiet, effective. He drops in my arms like a sack of feed.

I lower him into the mud, check for breath. Still alive. Just out.

I strip his earpiece and tuck it into my ear, adjusting the fit. Static first, then faint voices. Male, clipped, coordinating movement. They don't know I've taken one of theirs out of play. Good. That's leverage. Then I drag him to the shadows by the generator and tie his wrists and ankles with the spare zip tie from my belt pouch.

One down.

I scan the tree line, ears tuned for Elena's position. There's no more gunfire. That's either good news, or very bad.

I check my watch. Three minutes since she fired.

She should be headed back toward the cellar by now.

I move to intercept, circling the side yard. The other one will be heading toward me soon. Or toward her.

And I won't let him reach either of us.

Not tonight.

Not ever.

ELENA

The moment I hear the faint crunch of boots over wet grass, I know I'm not alone.

I'm halfway back to the cellar hatch, breath tight in my throat, when the shadows shift near the tree line to my right. I freeze, press flat to the earth behind the stacked wood pile that conceals the entrance.

A figure moves through the mist. He's slower than the others and more deliberate. Like he's in charge.

I grip the Glock tighter, let out a slow breath. My braid sticks to the back of my neck. Mud clings to my elbows and knees. This isn't combat on a field. This is survival. Dirty, personal, unpredictable. It's not a battlefield, but it feels just as raw.

He stops three feet from the hatch, boot scraping the edge of the deck.

"Too quiet," he mutters. His voice is low, methodical. Not surprised. Not worried.

A voice crackles in his ear. I can't make out the words, but the man nods and lifts his weapon.

"Copy. Moving in."

I can't let him find the hatch. Not if Jack's plan is going to hold.

I rise slowly, Glock leveled at his back. "Drop it."

He turns. He doesn't appear startled, just curious. Almost amused.

"Well now," he says. "Didn't expect you to be this close."

"I said drop it."

He tilts his head, fingers twitching on the stock of his rifle. "You shoot me, and the others converge in thirty seconds. You really want to be the one that starts that clock?"

"I don't want to start it," I say evenly. "But I'll finish it."

A long pause.

Then, without warning, he spins.

I fire. The round hits his shoulder, jerking him off balance. He collapses onto one knee, weapon clattering from his hands.

He reaches for something else and I don't hesitate. I kick him hard in the chest, sending him backward into the mud.

"Don't."

This time, he listens.

I put my foot on his injured shoulder, pushing in with my boot on his injury as I roll him to his stomach. I place my knee between his shoulder blades as I pull his left arm back first, his body tensing from the pain of the bullet wound as I do. The pain helps subdue him. I zip-tie his wrists, then ankles, leaving him in a hog-tie position. It's tight, quick, and no slack. He curses under his breath but doesn't resist.

"You're gonna regret this," he growls.

"Already do," I mutter. I am not lying, I thought I left this world far behind.

He glares at me, teeth gritted, but he doesn't call out. Maybe he's too winded. Or maybe he knows backup isn't far and thinks he'll get his turn. I am not taking chances, I take my gun and hit him at the back of the skull, momentarily incapacitating him.

I scan the trees again. The woods feel too still now.

I duck down, ease open the hatch, and hesitate. I close the door then retreat for higher ground and tactical advantage instead.

Jack's still out there.

And I just took out the one who gave orders.

We better be ready for what's coming next.

JACK

The woods are too quiet.

That's the first thing I notice after the scuffle near the generator. No footsteps. No radio chatter. No rustling from boots against wet underbrush. It's the kind of silence that screams something's shifted.

I keep low, hugging the barn's shadow, AR drawn and earpiece still feeding me static. Whatever frequency they were using is dead. Either they're jamming their own signal or switching to silent comms.

I reach the side of the ranch house and press my back to the wall. From here, I can see the front porch. The same one I reinforced with spare fencing last year after a coyote slipped into the feed shed. A figure moves into view.

Not Elena.

Another man. Bulkier than the others, moving like he knows what he's doing. He checks corners, raises his weapon, scans high. Not a scout. A closer.

He reaches the porch steps and lifts one hand to signal someone behind him.

I don't wait.

I pivot from cover, aim, and fire twice. One shot hits the porch post, the second slams into his leg. He drops fast, cursing as his rifle skids across the wood.

I move quickly. Cross the yard in a sprint, shoulder down, boots thudding against soaked earth.

By the time he raises his sidearm, I'm on him.

We crash into the deck railing. His elbow clips my jaw, but I twist and slam him backward, using the momentum to pin him against the boards.

"You've got five seconds to tell me who sent you," I growl.

He sneers, blood on his teeth. "You already know."

I press the barrel to his collarbone. "Try me."

He hesitates. Then he smiles.

That's when I hear it, another click. Metal on metal. A second figure stepping onto the porch behind me.

Too late to turn.

I drop low as a shot cracks through the air. Wood splinters above my head.

ELENA

I've got a clear line of sight from the barn loft window. I made it here after neutralizing the intruder by the cellar. That was an adjustment from the original plan, but it gives me better visual over the house. Not much, but enough.

When I see the second man raise his weapon toward Jack, I don't think, I act.

I line up the shot, take one steady breath, and squeeze the trigger.

The window beside me vibrates with the echo. My target jerks back with a cry and tumbles sideways off the porch. He's hit and maybe not dead, but definitely out of the fight.

Jack doesn't miss a beat. He pivots and slams the man he's wrestling into the railing again, knocking the last of the fight out of him.

I keep the Glock trained on the porch, scanning for more movement. Nothing. Just the sound of heavy breathing. It's mine, cutting through the tension.

I duck back, heart pounding in my ears.

Every breath feels like it takes effort now. Not from fear, not entirely. From the weight of everything that almost happened. Of what still could.

Jack's alive. We are still standing.

But something tells me this was just the first wave.

And whoever sent them... won't take failure lightly.

I ease out of the barn loft and descend the narrow ladder into the shadowed stalls below. My legs shake slightly as I hit the ground, a delayed tremor from adrenaline wearing off. The barn creaks overhead, wind tugging at loose boards.

I duck behind a row of feed barrels, eyes adjusting to the dimness. A soft rustle draws my attention to the far end of the barn. I freeze.

A figure stands just inside the back entrance. He's tall, hood up, and unmoving.

My heart climbs into my throat.

But then he steps forward, arms raised slowly. Jack.

Relief crashes into me like a wave, but I don't let the Glock drop until I see his face in the slant of moonlight through the wall slats.

"We clear?" I whisper.

"For now," he says, voice low. "But they weren't the type to act alone. Someone else is pulling strings."

He crouches beside me, rifle angled toward the barn's entry.

"What do we do now?" I ask.

His jaw tightens. "We find out who sent them. And we make damn sure they regret it."

JACK

I sling the rifle and scan the barn's edge one more time before motioning Elena toward the back wall. We move in sync; quiet, low, and efficient. She's still wired from the fight, jaw tight, eyes sharp. And yet, something else is there too, a weariness beneath the fire. The kind that comes when you've been holding your breath too long.

"I checked the bodies," I murmur, crouching beside the stall door. "None of them had ID. Just burner comms and encrypted GPS trackers. Nothing useful."

She exhales, crouching beside me. "Professionals, then."

"Yeah. And not cheap."

She hesitates, then adds, "I took one down near the cellar. Didn't kill him. Hog-tied and tucked him out of sight."

I blink once, surprised. "You didn't mention that."

Didn't expect that. Maybe I underestimated her.

"Didn't have time," she says. "You were busy staying alive."

Fair enough.

A gust of wind rattles the barn roof. I glance up, then back to her. "The one you tied up… is he still conscious?"

She nods. "Might've cracked a rib or two."

"Good. He'll talk."

We head out into the open again, stepping over slick mud and shattered branches. The night's gone eerily calm, like the storm took everything noisy with it. But I know better. This quiet, it's just a pause.

At the edge of the porch, we stop. Two of the bodies are still where they fell. I kneel beside one, patting down the pockets carefully. A flash drive.

"Elena."

She's already crouched next to me. "What is it?"

"Could be nothing. Could be leverage." I turn it over once before tucking it into my vest. "We'll check it once we're inside."

But something about the feel of it, cold, clinical, familiar, it makes my gut twist. Declan used to carry drives like this. And when he did, they were never blank.

Elena's standing in the middle of the yard, her arms folded, face lit by moonlight.

"You ever think we'd end up here?" she asks.

I shake my head slowly. "Not like this."

She nods once, then turns back toward the house. Her steps are steady now, like something inside her has finally settled. Or maybe she's just bracing for what's next.

I follow, keeping watch. This team was probing defenses, this was not full-scale, not yet.

Because this isn't over.

Not by a long shot.

Chapter 8

A Guide Home

JACK

The sky's still dark, but the adrenaline has long since burned off. What's left is purpose. Focus. The kind that settles in after a fight, when your blood's cooled but your instincts haven't.

By first light, I've made the calls. Tom shows up first, hat crooked, thermos in one hand and a shotgun in the other. "Heard the ruckus," he says, voice low. "Figured you'd need backup."

"I needed it hours ago," I say, but there's no bite in it.

He nods to Elena, who stands beside me near the porch. "She alright?"

"She's still standing," I say.

The sheriff showed up just before sunrise, cruiser pulling onto the gravel like it had something to prove.

He asked the usual questions, "Did you get a look at them?" "Any license plate?" "Why would someone target you?"

I said as little as possible. Neither of us are hurt. No visible property damage. No footage since the power was cut.

He scribbled on his notepad like it mattered, but we both knew it didn't.

"You're not telling me everything," he said finally, eyes narrowing.

I didn't blink. "You're not wrong."

The sheriff sighed, closed his notebook, and left us with a promise to file a report we'll probably never see.

Shortly after, more trucks arrive. Locals from the feed store, a few from the volunteer firehouse. Lisa, Elena's friend, pulls up in her battered SUV, eyes sharp, already scanning the area like she's preparing for another wave.

Nobody asks questions. They just fan out across the property, sweeping the grounds, checking blind spots, locking gates. This town might bicker like family, but when danger shows up, we don't hesitate.

We watch the last of the intruders get hauled off by the sheriff's deputies, cuffed and still defiant.

Tom claps me on the shoulder. "You're not alone, you know. Not anymore."

I nod once. Words aren't my strong suit. Never have been.

Elena moves closer, her hand brushing mine. It's small, that contact. Quiet. But I feel it all the way down to the places I thought were still frozen.

We stand in silence as the last patrol truck disappears down the road.

The ranch is still.

For the first time since Declan died, it feels like ours again. Not just mine and not his memory either, but ours, in the way we always meant it to be. Back when he and I poured every extra dollar and every calloused hour into these fences, into the dream of building something lasting.

Back then, Elena was part of that too. She was there through the laughter, the long nights, the arguments over cattle placement and barn siding. When he died, it was like the whole thing fractured. She vanished into grief, and I buried myself in silence. The land kept growing, but the purpose behind it dried up.

But last night, side by side, we fought for it.

And somehow, standing here with her now, it feels right again. Like the ranch is no longer just a remnant of what we lost, but a foundation for what we might still build.

And that changes everything.

Later, the sun starts to spill gold across the fields, we don't say much. We don't need to. The air is damp and clean, the kind of calm that only comes after something wild and dangerous has passed through.

Elena and I sit on the back steps, boots muddy, hands wrapped around mismatched mugs of coffee. Steam curls up between us, quiet like the space we've earned.

She stares out across the pasture. Her braid's come half loose, wisps of hair clinging to her neck and cheek. "This place never felt like mine," she says softly. "Not after Declan. Not after everything."

I glance at her over the rim of my cup. "Felt the same way. Like we were both just ghosts walking around something we couldn't let go of."

She nods, eyes on the horizon. "But last night…"

"Last night," I echo, "we stopped being ghosts."

There's a long pause. The kind that should be awkward but isn't.

She shifts, resting her elbow on her knee. "Do you think he knew?"

"Declan?"

She nods. "That something was coming. That he'd built something too big to control."

I take a long sip. "If he did, he kept it buried. Buried too deep."

She doesn't say anything for a while. Just lets the silence wrap around us.

Then, without looking at me, she says, "Thank you. For believing in me. Even when I didn't deserve it."

My throat tightens. I want to tell her it wasn't belief; it was instinct. A gut pull that never really lets go.

Instead, I just nod. "Anytime."

The sun crests fully over the Rockies, painting the barn and fences in soft gold. Out in the distance, the Colorado plains roll out like waves, amber and endless, kissed by the light that lingers even as the sun tucks itself behind the towering silhouette of Pike's Peak.

It's a hundred acres of contrast. Trees near the heart of it, wild and wind-worn plains stretching out beyond, framed by the shadowed rise of the Rocky Mountains. From here, they look deceptively small, soft even. But I've stood at their base. I know how they rise like giants, the kind that inspired hymns and made you feel small in all the right ways.

This land. That is what brought Declan and me here in the first place. Before betrayal. Before silence. Back when it was about carving something honest out of the wild. It's the kind of place that holds your breath in the early morning and gives it back at dusk.

By mid-morning, the sky is a clear stretch of blue, washed clean by the storm. I tell Elena I've got something to show her, and we walk the short gravel path up toward the main gate.

The arch has been empty for years now. The ranch has had no name, no marker, just weathered beams that Declan and I once swore we'd stain and carve ourselves when the time was right. The stain never got bought. The carving never happened.

Until late last night.

I stop just short of the gate and nod toward the truck bed where the wooden sign rests, wrapped in a tarp. "Can you help me with that?"

She glances at it, then at me. "You've been working on something out here?"

"Had to make sure it felt right."

Together, we unroll the tarp. The cedar plank is smooth, the edges sanded clean. The words are burned deep, dark, and permanent:

TRUE NORTH RANCH

She stares at it for a long time. Her fingers trail over the woodgrain, slow and quiet, like she's reading more than just the words.

"Declan and I used to call it that when we were mapping out the fencing lines," I say. "He always said it felt like the only place that kept him steady."

She nods slowly. "He'd say things like that. Quietly, and usually when he thought no one was really listening." She hesitates, then adds, "I think this land gave him more peace than anything else ever did."

We hoist the sign together and hang it above the entry arch. It's a perfect fit. Like it belongs.

There's something final about the way it settles into place. It feels like slipping the last piece into a puzzle. It doesn't erase what we lost, but it frames it. Gives it shape. And standing here with her, steady and quiet, it feels like everything that's been broken might finally be finding its fit.

When we step back, the morning breeze stirs her blonde hair, and sunlight spills across the carved letters. It's as if the land itself is welcoming the name.

She reaches for my hand without looking, and I don't hesitate to take it.

"I think he'd like it," she whispers.

I nod. "I think he'd finally rest."

We stay there for a while, long enough for the breeze to settle and the weight in our shoulders to shift into something softer. Not gone, but lighter.

When we finally turn to head back, Elena pauses under the archway and glances at the sign one more time. I can see it in her expression; that same mix of ache and acceptance I've carried around for too long. But this time, we're not carrying it alone.

She slips her hand into mine again as we walk back toward the house, gravel crunching under our boots. The sun's riding higher now, but the way it stretches across the plains makes it feel like the day's still just beginning.

I glance sideways at her. "You thinking what I'm thinking?"

"That I might finally sleep without checking the locks three times?" she says, a half-smile tugging at her mouth.

"That too," I chuckle. "But also… maybe it's time to start figuring out what life looks like now."

She nods, quiet for a few steps then turns to me. "Together?"

"Yeah," I say. "Together."

She looks back, her smile soft now, more sure.

And I know that we're not just surviving anymore.

We're starting something. Something messy, maybe. Something uncertain. But ours. And whatever Declan left behind… we'll face it. But not blindly. Not again.

She leans against the porch post, eyes on the horizon. "So, what does this future look like?"

I shrug, half-smiling. "Quiet mornings. Fewer ambushes. Maybe some rebuilt trust."

She arches a brow. "And chickens?"

"If we must."

We both laugh. The laughter is light, and real. But it fades as the wind shifts.

Her face grows serious. "If this was just the first wave…"

I nod, jaw tightening. "Then we need to be ready for the second. That flash drive and envelope still sit on the counter, and T-6 is more than just a name. It's a warning."

She doesn't flinch and she doesn't look away.

And neither do I.

THE END.

If you enjoyed *Defending Elena,* then you will love *Disarming Elena.* Read chapter 1 on the very next page for a sneak peek.

Sneak Peek

True North Ranch Book 2

Disarming Elena

ELENA

The scent of kettle corn, dust, and hay hits me as soon as we step onto the rodeo grounds. I squint toward the grandstands where rows of families have gathered. The kids with painted faces, teens clustered under the shade of the snack tent, old-timers already settling into their usual spots like the past year hasn't passed at all.

Jack walks a step behind me, close but not quite touching. We've grown used to each other's rhythm, but we're not fully in step yet.

A month ago, I wouldn't have imagined standing beside Jack Harrison at the Harmony County Rodeo, wearing jeans that actually fit and a tucked-in flannel I borrowed from Lisa. She'd thrust it at me with a grin and the words, "Local color matters," like it was gospel. And maybe it is, out here. There's something about blending in that feels less like losing yourself and more like belonging. It's like you've earned a place at the table just by showing up and being real.

Lisa says it's about respect. "You don't walk into someone else's story wearing city edges," she told me once. I'm starting to understand what she meant. The dust on your boots, the right shade of denim, knowing when to nod instead of speak. It's not costume. It's connection.

Lisa's somewhere near the livestock pens, doing exactly what she always does; making sure no one goes unseen. She's probably rallying the 4H kids, telling them their goats deserve equal camera time as the barrel racers. That's Lisa: cheerleader, firebrand, and walking press release.

She's lived here her whole life and knows everyone's grandmother, birth order, and livestock rotation. But it's not just about knowing people, it's about *lifting* them. She's made it her mission to shine light on the overlooked corners of this county, whether it's a fourth-grade art show or a junior high stock auction. She says stories matter, especially the ones that don't make headlines. And the more time I spend around her, the more I believe she's right.

Maybe that's why I've found myself leaning into the quieter routines lately, the small things that wouldn't make the news but still matter. The past month hasn't been quiet, not by a long shot. The sheriff's department is still tracking leads on the men who came after us.

Jack spends most mornings reviewing maps and grainy satellite photos like a man who knows the next move is coming, just not when. I spend mine in the chicken coop. Or what will be a chicken coop once Tom helps me finish the fencing. It's my way of building something steady, one plank at a time. My way of creating a life that can't be stolen or shaken loose by fear.

Jack hasn't said no to the chickens, which, in his language, is practically a declaration of support.

He clears his throat beside me. "You sure you want to do this?"

I glance at the arena where the flag girls are warming up their horses, dust swirling around the hooves like smoke. "Attend the rodeo?"

"Be seen. Together."

I turn to look at him, sunlight catching in the graying temples of his dark hair. "We already fought off a small militia together. I think we can survive a few curious glances."

He huffs a laugh, then tips his cowboy hat lower over his eyes. "Rodeo crowd might be tougher."

I nudge his arm with mine. "We've handled worse." I smile slyly at him, catching his eyes for a moment.

He doesn't move away. "Yeah," he says quietly. "But this… this feels bigger somehow."

The weight in his voice isn't fear, it's hope. Cautious, hard-earned, but real. I reach for his hand. "Then let's be seen."

He huffs a laugh, slipping his hand into mine, intertwining our fingers.

Lisa waves us over to the bleachers she staked out earlier. Tom's already there, a foam cup of lemonade balanced on his knee, boots dusty and his usual grin in place.

"Took you two long enough," he says, nodding to the two open seats beside him. "Was beginning to think the chickens came between you."

Jack lifts a brow at me. "Told you it was a bad idea to share my coffee with them."

"You're the one who started naming them," I fire back as I sit.

Tom chuckles, then leans toward me. "He named one Nugget," I laugh as I say it.

"Because she pecked through the feed sack like a drill sergeant," Jack mutters. "She's got spirit."

Lisa sits down with a bag of popcorn, giving me a sidelong smile. "You two planning on opening a bed and breakfast for barn animals, or are we going to get updates on the real stuff?"

The real stuff.

I glance around, scanning the crowd. No sign of danger. No shadows lurking behind the grandstands or out by the trailers. Still, I keep my phone in my pocket, set to silent but buzzing every few hours with an encrypted message from Sam, our reluctant informant. He hasn't revealed much yet, just hints. Symbols. Warnings. But it's enough to keep me watchful.

Jack must sense the shift in my body because his hand brushes mine. It's nothing overt, just the edge of his knuckle grazing mine like an anchor.

There's something kind in the way Jack makes space for me. And something steady in the way I find myself stepping into it. We've both agreed: whatever's growing between us needs to be real. Built slow. Honest.

We've barely held hands. There's too much to work through, too many tangled threads still hanging between the past and what might be next. But we both seem content to take it slow. To let the silence fill in where words aren't ready. Whatever this is becoming, it doesn't need to be hurried.

I'm back in my old room, Declan's room. It feels both normal and not. The walls are familiar, the rhythm of the ranch settling into something that feels like home again. And yet, there's a shift I can't ignore. A quiet awareness, like a small ember lit deep in my chest. It stirs every time Jack walks into a room or stands a little too close. He doesn't push. Neither do I.

Sometimes, late at night, I hear his boots on the porch, pacing. Other times, he leaves a mug of tea outside my door. We're not rushing anything. After what we both came through, trust is the most valuable thing we've got.

A cheer erupts as the rodeo announcer calls the start of the first event; junior roping. The kids are all elbows and nerves, their horses twitchy under the bright banners.

"Feels almost normal," Jack murmurs beside me, like he's afraid to name it too soon.

I smile, watching a girl no older than ten wrangle a calf like it's the most important thing she'll ever do. "It feels like hope."

He nods.

The sun is hot, the dust clings to everything, and still, I feel steady. Like maybe, just maybe, we've earned this quiet moment.

But the fire isn't over. Not yet. And whatever comes next, we won't face it alone.

To get the next book, *Disarming Elena,* find it at your favorite book retailer, or scan the QR code below.

And if you feel so inclined, please leave a review of the book on your favorite book platform.

Thank you!

Follow along on social media or visit TessaLeighBooks.com to discover the next book in the series and explore all available titles by Tessa Leigh.

True North Ranch Series:

Defending Elena

Disarming Elena

Courting Elena

Women's Domestic Fiction

The Plans They Made Together

Coming 2026:

Second Chance Romance Series:

Plans Changed

ABOUT THE AUTHOR

Tessa Leigh grew up immersed in the rhythms of military life, moving from place to place, gathering stories and experiences like souvenirs. Surrounded by a family of storytellers shaping her world view, she developed an early love for narratives that explores resilience, transformation, and the unseen connections between people.

A lifelong traveler, Tessa Leigh believes that stories should move the heart and challenge the mind with the ability to transport readers to places both familiar and unknown. Her work blends layered storytelling with thematic depth, crafting worlds where escape and reinvention intertwine.

When not writing, she can be found with her family dreaming up their next adventure to inspire her next artistic endeavor.

Find more information at TessaLeighBooks.com